Fiddle Lane

Johns Hopkins: Poetry and Fiction
John T. Irwin, General Editor

Poetry Titles in the Series

John Hollander, *"Blue Wine" and Other Poems*

Robert Pack, *Waking to My Name: New and Selected Poems*

Philip Dacey, *The Boy under the Bed*

Wyatt Prunty, *The Times Between*

Barry Spacks, *Spacks Street: New and Selected Poems*

Gibbons Ruark, *Keeping Company*

David St. John, *Hush*

Wyatt Prunty, *What Women Know, What Men Believe*

Adrien Stoutenberg, *Land of Superior Mirages: New and Selected Poems*

John Hollander, *In Time and Place*

Charles Martin, *Steal the Bacon*

John Bricuth, *The Heisenberg Variations*

Tom Disch, *Yes, Let's: New and Selected Poems*

Wyatt Prunty, *Balance as Belief*

Tom Disch, *Dark Verses and Light*

Thomas Carper, *Fiddle Lane*

Fiddle Lane

Thomas Carper

The Johns Hopkins University Press

Baltimore and London

This book has been brought to publication
with the generous assistance of the Albert Dowling Trust.

The Johns Hopkins University Press
701 West 40th Street
Baltimore, Maryland 21211-2190
The Johns Hopkins Press Ltd., London

Ⓧ
The paper used in this book meets the minimum
requirements of American National Standard
for Information Sciences—Permanence of Paper
for Printed Library Materials, ANSI z39.48-1984.

Library of Congress Cataloging-in-Publication Data

Carper, Thomas.
Fiddle Lane / Thomas Carper.
p.   cm. — (Johns Hopkins, poetry and fiction)
ISBN 0-8018-4268-9 (alk. paper).
— ISBN 0-8018-4269-7 (pbk. : alk. paper).
I. Title. II. Series.
PS3553.A7625F5   1991
811'.54—dc20   91-17652

For Janet

Contents

III. *Observations*

I

Beginnings

Creation

Three thousand million years — six syllables
Restore to us the world where words began,
Where, linked like sounds, harmonious molecules
Combined to build the building blocks of man.
The steaming seas, swept by electrical storms,
Became a womb for beauty that would grow
As ever more elaborated forms
Made up a mind, and all a mind could know.
Eons of measure on a rocky beach,
Ages of symmetry in flashing skies
At last were brought to meaning in the speech
A singular, mindful creature would devise
To let an ordered human world begin
The passionate story of its origin.

The Monster in the Park

No wonder eyes are vacant, and the snout
Softly puffed. The terror has been tamed.
The wings crush on the shoulders where the stout
Body hunches, seemingly ashamed
Of having once ruled vast interior space,
Great darknesses where it had grown to be
The master image for an ancient race,
Guarding the entrances to mystery.
Now in this pretty park the monster seems
Only an ornament that we admire
As sculpture, or consider, like our dreams,
As imaging some primitive desire
Which, having lived until its ways were known,
Looked on an ordered world and turned to stone.

Daedalus Invents God

To Daedalus was ascribed the invention of the axe and saw. It was he, they said, who first fixed arms and legs to the *xoana*, the shapeless primitive statues of the gods.

— New Larousse Encyclopedia of Mythology

His worship never left him satisfied.
The rites he followed ended in a void.
That God did have a form, no one denied,
But no one working wood or stone employed
Sufficient insight to reveal those lines —
Being content to show "mysterious powers"
With lumpish, inarticulate designs
Priests would set up amid their flames and flowers.
What was the mystery? Where could it reside?
The artist pondered, then with axe and saw
Fashioned a father's image out of pride
In his own lineage, shaping a new law.
When he had made the last cut in the wood,
He rested, knowing that his work was good.

In the Garden

Adam and Eve, now in their seventieth year,
Not tempted, never fallen, day by day
Kept, as the Lord commanded, out of fear,
A careful distance from the forbidden tree.
Laboring together, they subdued
The raw, luxuriant flowers that pushed up
Into well-ordered rows, and cut the rude
Wet thrusts of green that seemed to make them slip
On grassy paths. One morning, when their prayer
Had offered usual thanks, and, hearts at peace,
They went to labor, an inexplicable stare
Touched with surprise the ever-attentive Eve,
Who shook as Adam showed his obedient wife
The tinge of blight upon the tree of life.

A Workable Guillotine

O Gargi, do not ask too much, lest thy head should fall off.
Thou askest too much about a deity about which we are not to ask
too much.

— *Brihadaranyaka Upanishad*

Do not ask about the god, but ask
About the fruit and seed, about the rind
Cast off. Question the kernel and the husk,
And notice how the lily is designed
For — what? She too deserves your inquiry,
Who sits alone not reading in her book,
Tired at day's end. Then surmise why he
Looks puzzled at you, as if you mistook
Some meaning of a word. Exhaust the stars
With counting; measure to an atom's length
Each footstep; calculate the millibars
Pressing upon you. If you still have strength
Ask, finally: "What always is denied?"
And then the god will be identified.

The Cosmos

Eons ago, they say, it all began
At one point, smaller than the eye can see,
And from that point continues to expand
In ever-emptier infinity.
I partly can believe it. I am here
In an established cosmos, having grown
From tiny points. But I do not endure
A motion always outward and alone:
I ring and spiral steadily with a few
Who have become my firmament of care,
Where subtle forces constantly renew
A faith that we have something yet to share
Though all the universe's atoms move
Toward regions desolate of human love.

Casting the Nets

It must be in the evening, for our boat
Rides fragilely on the water; if a wave
Should lap over a gunnel, the remote
Reaches of river would become a grave.

Yet in the calm after the winds of day,
We move out, confident, and do not break
The almost-silence as we row away
From shore, tipping the arrow of our wake.

A hand thrust through the surface feels the force
Of currents that oppose; a dragonfly
Inquires of us, then takes a different course
And disappears into the yellow sky.

When we arrive, the land is lost in mist.
We balance carefully as we prepare
The nets whose spidery strands seem to resist
Their being flung extravagantly in air.

But, brought to standing height and artfully
Swirled out into the sunset, they begin
To wing and fan as though infinity
Could be encompassed, caught, and gathered in.

II

In Families

A Picture of the Reverend's Family with the Child of One

Particularly at the left side of his face,
As you face him, the line is so distinct
You might suppose the negative was inked
To heighten contrasts. I am in my place,
But all my shadows blend into his clothes
Where hardly a button shows, they are so black.
My father's right hand rests on Mother's neck.
The parted curtains at the left disclose
A sunlit bowl with fruit and gourds — perhaps
Real ones. The fluid drape of Mother's dress
Softens the chaste and angular plainness
Of this memorial scene, where in their laps
I reach up past my boyish-girlish curls
To his priest's collar and her string of pearls.

The Tree Seat

Each time I took my place, there was a glow
Of green vibrating from the leaves in light;
The sun arranged itself so it could show
I was its golden focus at the height
Of summer noons. The forest had prepared
That grand seat I ascended as my throne,
While every soaring woodland songster shared
News of the kingdom. I was not alone
Amid the colored musics, and my heart
Beat to their rhythms; my new eyes could see
The pulsing brightnesses that would be part
Of building up my possibility;
Though, from the distant house would come the mild
Voices reminding me to be a child.

Mickey

Mother must have heard the thumpy landing,
Then silence, then my glee. When she arrived
At the high stairwell, Mickey roused himself,
Checked himself for damage, arched his back,
And walked away. I smiled down through the bars
Of the upstairs banister from which the cat
Had clumsily taken off, with my assistance,
To interact originally with the air —
To make himself an aeronautical cat,
A cat entirely changed from what he was:
Rug cat, chair cat, bed cat, usual cat.
Mother was not pleased. I think she spanked me.
A few days later, spring had opened windows
And from the second floor, now self-propelled,
Mickey sailed into the afternoon
Effortlessly gliding to the garden.
Now, is this story one of primitive
Sadistic impulse on my part, or one
Of that small creature learning joy in flight?

Tom and Stone

Like everyone, I'm bothered by those pictures
The relatives have gathered, and then give you
Just when you think you've got your life in order.
The album pages, early black and white
Snapshots (you're the baby), colored ones
Of teenage summer outings, with the colors
Fading in that disconcerting way,
Those painful, handsome studies of your parents
Made by photographers who signed their work
(How many of us will be living next year?),
And then the mystery prints. Who are those strangers?
This morning, going through that envelope,
I found among my many selves a three-year
Me, posed solemnly (in North Carolina,
In the Fletcher churchyard where I played then)
Before what looks most like a Celtic menhir,
A stone on end, and twice the height that I am,
Which, if I ever bothered to go back there,
Would still be just as it was then, still standing.

Bedtime

He curls into the warm spot he has made,
Picturing the darkening house below,
Alert as ritual noises rise and fade.
The kitchen light snaps off. He sees a glow
From the gas stove bluing the white walls.
Machinery ceases in the sewing room.
A volume drops in place on the study shelves.
The steam pipes ring as coal is shoveled in
The furnace, whose door clanks shut. And now, at last,
Separate steps are sounding on the stair.
He draws his knees up tightly to his chest,
Repeating phrases from an early prayer,
And shuts his eyes — as if anticipating
A time of sleep, and not a time of waiting.

Turning in Bed

The stench of early cruelty returns
As I, a child, crouch underneath low boughs
Playing with candles. In small pans the worms
Writhe. Now I grow, and from a neighbor's house
He runs at me, screaming that I have hid
His toy gun, which I get and, with a blow
That terrifies me, smash it to his head,
Causing blood and my blinding tears to flow.
The picture breaks. I ache. The sheets are taut.
I turn for comfort, then return to hell,
Fleeing across a fiery space and caught
By images assaulting me until
I fear I will not wake again, but keep
Revolving painfully on the spit of sleep.

Catching Fireflies

Into warm evenings on a shadowy road
The children ventured, and once more they knew
Remarkable hours, when points of darkness glowed
With fresh surprise as myriad fireflies drew
Each to imagine stars, but stars at hand,
Come down to share a fragrant earthly night,
Freed from a rigid beauty in that band
Turning eternally with chilly light;
Come down to be the stars that they could hold,
Could cup in secret space their fingers made,
Making a center for a little world
That, when some sign might hint that it might fade,
Could open like a universe, and there
Restore the lightning to the summer air.

Her Diamond Ring

She realized the glittering stones were glass,
Though he, it seemed, would keep her unaware
About so much. The setting might be brass
As well, though washing, ironing, constant care
For all the clothes she folded into piles
And put in drawers had brought a deepening
Glow to the metal, so the children's smiles
Were no surprise. "Oh, what a pretty ring,"
They told her when it sparkled in the light,
And she would murmur, "Diamonds," for she knew
That her display of elegance was right
For them to keep in memory as they grew
To know how such rings might be symbols of
What can be realized from troubled love.

Hide-and-Seek

In the large living room the game began.
Bubby would close his eyes, and then would call
The solemn numbers loudly as she ran
Into their father's study, or the hall,
Hiding herself, but hoping to be found.
He always found her — trembling with delight
When he would move the door, or come around
Behind the chair. Then she recalled the night
When she became an only child, the day
Bubby was placed before the fireplace,
Before being taken finally away,
When she had stood tiptoe to touch his face
And turned to Mother, sure she should be told:
"Bubby needs a blanket now. He's cold."

New Life

At first the doctor's words didn't make sense.
The two were well. And yet something was wrong.
"This kind of problem has its precedents,
And, in time, Johnny can be nursed along;
At least he isn't . . . ." So John grew in strength
To stare at us, or soil his pants, or howl
A strange, banshee-like howl, until at length
I dreaded home. I didn't have a soul,
Somebody told me. "Courage," I replied. . . .
For on a summer afternoon he sat
Within his rubber pool: I saw him slide
Flailing — as he did everything. The fat
Bubbles rose glimmering up as I gazed down . . .
Then snatched him back, afraid to let him drown.

The First-born

With Mother in bed, calling it "Doctor's order,"
But flat out, really, to curse him, play in the yard
Is hourly more aimless. Making water
On her petunias, which he'd do when hard
Pressed for revenge, gives no relief. They paste
Their rough leaves to the ground, and warmly smell
When blasted by the jet. But still the taste
Of exile from her odor seems to dwell
Upon his tongue. Inside, a negligee
Covers the breasts he thinks of, while below
A bulge hills up the sheet. This is the way
Exquisite punishments are fashioned — slow,
And absolutely certain to arrive.
He kicks a stone, hating to be alive.

A Portrait of Paul in 1897

The sailboat on the floor is sailing away
From the painting's center, where a forlorn boy,
Who, at five-and-a-half, has outgrown play,
Seems to wonder why anyone put a toy
Into his frame. Enduring the wide-brimmed hat
And sailor-suitish outfit which set him apart
From children without portraits, conscious that
His image will become a work of art,
Paul thinks of how the window's light must make
A shadow on the flowery wall behind him,
Of how the woman, painting, will mistake
The thoroughness of his effort, and remind him
Not to fidget, and please to keep his eyes
Steady — as though *he* hoped for some surprise.

Bumper Cars

The skinny, clean-cut kid in the red shirt,
With a giggly pal beside him, steers away
From random pileups, as if it would hurt
His pride to mix too easily in the fray
Others are making. Driving skillfully,
He circles at top speed, keeping his eye
On a young couple's car that aimlessly
Nudges and prods at cars of friends going by.
The music blares and lulls. Then, suddenly,
The clean-cut kid, as if he'd taken aim,
Swerves toward the boy and girl and violently
Slams into them. Their looks of almost pain
And puzzlement are met with a slight grin
As he backs up, to circle once again.

Wedding Feast

Everybody is related to him —
His uncle, singing dirty songs, the bride,
The whole hall full, the ugly, prissy cousin
Some aunt connived to get put by his side.
They're clapping now. It's Father's turn. He rises
Unsteadily, and starts by reeling off
The crude priest-spinster joke his son despises.
Studying grease stains on the tablecloth
He ducks his head down, but she sees it. "Paul,
Your dad is great. I think you should be proud."
She touches him; he draws away. His soul
Is, as he feared, under attack. Aloud,
He murmurs, "I am," trying to resign
Himself. At last the waiter comes with wine.

Catechism Class

"But why then, Father, do the children die?"
For weeks the newspapers have written of
The Ethiopian famine. He asks why
A God permits these deaths if God is Love.
The priest regards him warily. He tries
To frame an answer. While the moments pass
Silently, the intelligence in the eyes
Of this boy lets him see, as through a glass,
Jesus sitting in the temple where
The doctors are astonished as he speaks.
The question is impossible. But there,
Before him, is an earnest child who seeks
A reasoned faith, and who will find it odd
When all his answers end with "God is God."

New Home

Darkness upon the river in midsummer.
Play in turbulence under the ledge
With other boys is, for the newcomer,
The crucial test. Upstream, beyond the bridge,
The factory where his father works sends up
Transparent smoke into the morning air,
While in the brown house on the distant block
His mother now, perhaps, is wondering where
Her child has gone. The swirls about his waist
Are angry. Sharply edged stones pain his steps.
The shouts become less friendly. He has placed
His new life in their hands. His footing slips;
Then, kicking wildly, buoyed by his pride,
He starts in terror for the other side.

The Inseparables at the Rink

The three hang out together. Angular,
Intense, and devious, the first displays
The best technique, skates strongest, is aware
Of every motion's meaning, every phrase
He mocks the second with, the suffering one
Required, although awkward on the ice,
To be there to endure the unconcern
Of their best friend — the third, who in each race
Beats both — with one unwilling to prevail.
The victor smiles his soft smile when they shove him
Playfully, glad to touch. He cannot fail
With such as these to serve him, and to love him.
As minutes pass, the polished steel blades hiss
Through loops and circles. Life will be like this.

The country's miles on miles of interminable plain
Go by like school days under cloudy skies
Until, one dawn, while watching from the train,
I see the West arrive. The mountains rise
Golden with promise for new life to come.
There, at the ranch, for the first time I ride
Not with a master, but a companion,
A stable boy my age for friend and guide
Through hours of afternoon. Up hill and down,
Across hot fields and woodlots, we explore
A country that seems more and more my own.
Thirsty, we find a house where, by the door,
A water faucet on a stanchion stands
To fill, as with a blessing, our cupped hands.

The Coach

He lined us up and called me out. Half-drunk
At three o'clock that afternoon, he stood
Breathing his stink at me, spouting some bunk
About my character. I was no good
Because I skipped the practices I hated
And went delivering papers with a friend.
There in the stench his slurring words created
I waited for the ridicule to end.
While my fellow players, like me wearing
Neanderthal football gear, looked at the ground
Or curiously at him sideways, I was staring
Toward that strange adult face with a profound
Conviction that I would not play again
For this man who was here to make us men.

J-Strip

Gunned in reverse, the car speeds off downhill
Backward. The driver slams it into "drive."
The tires shudder, start to spin; their squeal
Shrills across fields. The minute is alive
With power. As the tread begins to melt
In its near-midnight heat, a smoking strip
Smears the road's surface — a black, stinking belt
Of rubber. Slowly the tires get a grip
Again, the car accelerates, then stops.
Now they will see their work. The headlights trace
An arc when turning: trees, a fence, the tops
Of rocks, the J-strip permanently in place.
They drink to it, and crumpled cans are thrown
To glint in moonlight after they are gone.

The Solemn Son

"It's his." They'll weigh it out behind the store.
Harry Nason writes the boy's name, Steve
Burnell. The boy looks solemnly at the floor,
Trying to work it out. It's hard to believe
That in one deafening moment in the woods,
At daybreak, as he shivered from the cold,
So much could change. He overhears his dad's
Words as Harry has the story told.
"Two shots . . . the heart." He'd hardly time to see
The buck before the crashing blasts that killed
Him rang in his ears so overpoweringly
That just when he was sure he'd be fulfilled
He felt dazed and deserted. Now the son
Hears Harry's voice from miles away. "Well done."

Facts

It is important that a son should know
His role, and should be told the woman's role,
And know it is effeminate to show
Emotion, or the least lapse of control
That might mean caring for another man —
Even a father. "Never say, 'I love
You,'" I was told. If ever tears began
After an argument, he would reprove
Me mockingly: "Only fags cry." The first
Time that he said this to me, I misheard
The slangy phrase, but knew my tears were worst
Of possible betrayals. Yet that word
Stays with me, and when my father shall die,
No man will weep because only facts cry.

Vita

If only I had been properly born!
Delivered in some clinic off the Bowery,
Brought home by my abandoned mom through trash
In streets and hallways, up to the fifth-floor
Infested flat, one bed, a broken chair,
A hot plate for the water I was washed in.
And raised in terror of the local gangs
Who'd rip off my lunch money, and the toughs
Who'd trail me to the dingy school library
To tear my papers up, and break my glasses.
Then I could have held my head up proudly.
"Yes, it was hard. But with my mom's devotion,
And the kind priest's, who read me Shakespeare's sonnets,
I got the grades that got me into Harvard.
From there, you know the story." Oh heroic
Me, then — not the little gentleman
Who started private school in kindergarten,
Was pampered and indulged, and praised for trifles,
And given most of what he thought he wanted.

Milkweed

A light toss sends them clouding into air
Over her head. Thousands of tiny seeds
Drawn from the pods are suddenly everywhere,
Their manyness miraculous in a breeze
That sweeps about us with an autumn chill
To swirl the wispy plumes round and around,
Dizzying eyes that follow them, until
After their flight they settle to the ground.
Alice is enthralled — so small an act
Has made a marvel of the sunlit sky;
To know that on each fragile stalk is packed
Such glory is this day's discovery,
As milkweed opens amiably to please
A child amid her possibilities.

That's a Nice Leg

She's nine and worried. That midsummer day
We who were guests had left the dining room
After breakfast, a few had gone to play
Tennis, and I was thinking of a swim.
Lisa had her suit on, and was standing
Next to me, so we talked. "You've been here often?"
"Just twice." "Will you be going to the landing?"
"When Mommy comes." Perhaps my voice did soften
When I said, "That's a nice lake," for she heard
"A nice leg," and with ages-old concern
Pressed hers, and declared it fat. My word,
"Lake," repeated, caused her eyes to turn
Downward — as though a blossom could be bent
On closing from its own embarrassment.

He had been hurt. He'd called me to the fence
Early that morning, but I hadn't gone.
Perhaps donkeys have something of human sense;
The greeting unreturned left him alone.
At noon he stood, as usual, at his wall,
His head against it, keeping away the flies.
Three times I called, with no response at all,
Or movement. I began to realize
He was as desolate as I'd often been
When failing to make my affection clear,
And so I walked quite humbly up to him,
And spoke it slowly in his donkey ear.
I didn't know if he would understand.
Later, he came and took bread from my hand.

Aïda at the Sink

I have been over into the future, and it works.
            — Lincoln Steffens, after visiting Russia in 1919

"Cold" is the only operating spigot,
Yet water is quite warm this summer morning.
My fellow camper takes a plate, to stick it
Into his sudsy dishpan while performing
A dance upon its surface with a sponge —
The accompaniment, an aria from Aïda
Whistled vigorously as the grunge
Dissolves in Lux. He must have had to feed a
Small battalion for so many dishes
To be so soiled. And now, a beautiful
Teenage girl approaches with delicious
Verve, surprising her papa. The dutiful
Whistler, caught in mid-crescendo, smirks.
I have seen the present, and it works.

A Story in Verse

The story has stayed with him down the years.
When eight, the hundred lines were learned with ease.
And now almost a lifetime disappears;
He lives once more in early memories.

He tells how the Canadian, Trudeau,
Leaves for the States, abandoning his friends,
Grows rich, then loses everything, and so
Comes home, forgiven, as the story ends.

Traces of local accent re-create
Performances eight decades in the past
When all his family would celebrate
As Mr. Waterhole returned at last.

The storyteller's eyes betray a yearning
To be again at home. Then, a returning.

Her voice is childlike. "No man lives forever,
Dead men rise up never . . . ." Looking at me,
Her eyes are bright. "But even the weariest river,"
My mother sighs, "winds somewhere safe to sea."
Sitting across the table, gaunt and small,
She murmurs, "I remember," as though I
Should praise her, as in school. She can recall
Only fragments from a history
That stopped, it seems, some fifty years ago —
Before my birth. The ruin of her mind
Is infinite. She says, "I do not know
Just who you are, but you are very kind."
Then, after a pause, "I'm very glad you came."
She smiles and calls me by my father's name.

A Conversation

It must have been there from the start. Recall
The way she was with Father — never aware
Of his caged-animal look when pushed to the wall
In some dispute that made us children stare.
And how she ruled the help, or dealt with those
Of Father's business friends she could not choose.
The way her ultimatums would dispose
Of arguments she did not wish to lose.
Do you remember when we took that drive
When she was in her eighties, and we saw,
Off to the right, a great white heron dive
With such perfection we were both in awe,
And how we stared, astonished, as she said,
"You know I do not choose to turn my head"?

Pick Up Your Belongings on the Way Out

I thought the package would be larger: shoes
Not thoroughly broken in, though scuffed and stained;
Wrinkled a bit and now drab-seeming clothes;
The wallet with a few bills, and some change;
The watch, stopped, with its pretty gold case scarred
Where it had struck the pavement when I tripped
While running, in my twenties, and hit hard,
Scraping my forearm on cement; a ripped
Ticket to a show; a calendar–
Appointment book for years back; photographs
Of old friends in forgotten spots, that are
Fading to yellow; pencils; a few scraps
Of paper — poems; and several family
Letters, never opened, meant for me.

Leaving

Leaving the home they built together, they
Went slowly by a field where memory
Ran with them through an afternoon at play,
And where one day a single chickadee
Swayed on a stalk, poking about for seed
While one had hushed the other, and a look
Brought a delight to both. Beside the bed,
Now dry, where in the spring a little brook
Flowed vigorously, they paused, almost as though
Even now they heard a delicate melody
Of water carrying off the glittering snow.
Their seasons had been here. They turned to see
That landscape one more time; then, like the dead,
With blank and resolute faces looked ahead.

I Am Just the Same

> I am just the same as when
> Our days were a joy, and our paths through flowers.
>   — Thomas Hardy

A world in pieces with the loved one gone.
The garden failing and the house a chill.
The bedroom a despair to look upon,
With flowers dying at the window sill.
Pictures of the places where no more
Two can be two are desolate in their frames.
The faithless clock ticks as it ticked before
They met in love and vowed to join their names.
Gazing about, he feels the urgent force
Of recent wishes rise up when her name
Comes to his lips, as though that great divorce
Had never happened. "I am just the same,"
He wants to tell her, passionately; "I lack
Youth only — and the hope to have you back."

III

Observations

The Dump Man

The Dump Man is fastidious. He insists
That bottles for his barrels show no trace
Of what was in them once, and he resists
Your setting large ones in a separate place.
As for the newspapers, they must be tied
In neatly squared-off bundles, but you need
Not have the dates in order, or decide
On pages he should read: he cannot read.
The boxes, wrappings, scraps of meat, the rinds,
The wilted flowers, fish heads, skin and bone
Go straight into the burner. If he finds
You dawdling at the pit, he'll move you on,
Because the Dump Man has the final say
When anything that's used is thrown away.

What People Make

It's a little hard to explain to my friends at first what I do. They
don't understand that people make kazoos.
> — John Battaglia, in the *New York Times*

They make wars, babies, sonnets, money, haste,
Fantastic visions, patent leather shoes,
Pledges to keep, paper towels to waste,
Long recipes for life and oyster stews,
Thick books contrived for everybody's taste,
Slim volumes only doting authors choose,
New glasses for the old when they're replaced,
And awkward pauses anyone can use.
For people stuck on sticking, they make paste;
For people stuck on answers, they make clues;
For people just plain stuck, or who are faced
With failure, they make big bottles of booze;
And for those seeking simply to amuse
Themselves a moment, people make kazoos.

On Sitting Down to Read the Dust Jacket Once Again

Phoebus, what talent! When she turns her lyre on
"A thousand hearts beat happily." — Lord Byron

"What oft was thought" is here, but who could hope
For such expression? — Alexander Pope

This philosophic poetry is built on
Rock, not sand. The sheep are fed. — John Milton

One of the smooths! Her supple poems permit one
To love an unbarbaric yawp. — Walt Whitman

Positive capability completes
These "symbols of a high romance." — John Keats

No reader on these roads is ever lost;
Her words make "all the difference." — Robert Frost

Success is sweet. This poet has begun
To taste its liquor. — Emily Dickinson

The Young Narcissus

Tiresias prophesied that Narcissus would live to be old if he never came to know himself.

He knew something about his heritage
But never freely mentioned it to friends;
If some kid called him "bastard," he would rage,
Threatening to kill him with his own bare hands.
He knew his pluck and cunning could achieve
For him, one day, a more than local fame;
Even now, chance comments led him to believe
That neighbors nodded when they heard his name.
Once, hunting, in his element, he strayed
Into a little hollow. Looking down,
He saw an image in a pool. Dismayed,
He hesitated — then turned back to town
Telling himself he would refuse to draw
Conclusions about what he thought he saw.

Ill in Babylon

In ancient Babylon almost everyone was a physician. Sick persons were exhibited in the market place, and it was the duty of all passers-by to discuss the patient's symptoms with him on the chance that they themselves or someone they knew had survived a similar malady.

— "Medicine," *Columbia Encyclopedia*

Some speak with lepers, those with minds deranged,
The palsied, or the epileptics. I
Stand here amid the market stalls, estranged
By physical health and sick philosophy.
Were I to go to the authorities
And say to them, "I must be put on view;
The nation must examine my disease,
Dissect my thoughts, prescribe what I must do,"
Would they look blankly at me, and in scorn
Send me away as one spoiled by luck?
Or would their gazes wander off from mine
As if they too had seen into the dark
When on an ordinary market day
They stopped to heal, but found nothing to say?

Dante in the Market

The bells begin above the city square.
The reverent, leading children by the hand,
Mount the church steps into a solemn air
And vanish. Dante, at a market stand,
Hears the faint singing. Early-morning clouds
Are breaking up; a wave of sunlight pours
Over the vivid awnings and the crowds
Dressed brightly for the holiday outdoors.
He is here for honey, bread, and wine
Without a thought that he will soon be served
By an enchanting girl who, with a fine
Talent for leaving those she likes unnerved,
Will press the coin in change into his hand
With just that pressure he will understand.

Basho's Journey

My body was escaping me. My arm
Ached with its easy burden; on my back,
Which had for weeks obediently borne its pack,
Pain settled like a stone. In my alarm
I dreaded a defeat along the way
To the extreme north, where my pilgrimage
Was, I thought, destined. How could I engage
Such fear? At last I brought myself to say
That all was providence, and, even lame,
I might go on a little. When I trod
As firmly as I could, my strength renewed
And miles were put behind me; so I came
At last into the north, and could lie down —
A body that I knew to be my own.

A Couple in the Café de la Gare

She cannot be his daughter, for he turns
Her face toward him with gestures of a lover
To kiss her on the mouth. But her concerns
Seem deeper than his caring will discover,
For, after kissing, she brings to her lips
The coffee cup, and lets the white rim press
More than a moment on her tongue. She sips
At last. He seems aware of a distress
He cannot touch. Her gaze now, like his own,
Is blankly toward the wall, the bar, the glasses,
The bottles, and the mirror. They have known
Such moments in the past. An engine passes,
Cars pass, so they collect their things and rise
To go, not looking in each other's eyes.

Burning Her Past

He would have her. But she had herself,
In part, locked in a chest of drawers. The key
Was on a ring hung from a kitchen shelf
In plain sight, so could not with secrecy
Be hidden away, or lost. And so she knew
When he possessed it, when his hands attacked
The boxes with the photographs, and threw
The letters to the floor, and then ransacked
The farthest corners; when he made the fire
And sent the life she had before they met
Violently into it — as if desire
For him would let her willingly forget
All that was not himself, simply because
No trace remained of anything she was.

Nobody at Treblinka

Sie waren nicht ein kleiner Mann.
      — Film director Claude Lanzmann to a former
         Nazi official

But keep the scale in mind. What single man
Could undertake that kind of enterprise
When each day trains from half of Europe ran
Into the camp? The prisoners swarmed like flies
Onto the platforms. Hundreds did their jobs
Of keeping books, processing and selecting,
Or guarding work brigades, or moving mobs
Into the chambers . . . cleaning . . . disinfecting.
You see, with those large numbers, no one said,
"X is responsible." We were a team
Handling the hordes — the living, and the dead.
Mine was a minor function. Do I seem
Like someone who would cause such sufferings?
I was a nobody. Nobody does those things.

Narcissus at the Seashore

He leans back on his elbows on the beach,
Heels in the wavelets, gazing at the sea.
The islands in the haze are out of reach.
About him, though, summer activity
Peoples his musing. In the larger waves
A sailor trims his boat's sail to the wind,
Working from shore. Nearby, a young child braves
The shifting waters, helped by a deeply tanned
Woman, sensuous in the spray. Each one
Attracts him and reflects him. He will turn
To see you in the crowd, as though alone,
And will suppose such intimate concern
That, even lacking any sense of you,
His eyes will say it: "You must love me, too."

Hope

Some say she triumphs like a summer breeze
Progressing easily through crowded streets
To lift oppression and anxieties,
And touch with blessing everyone she meets.
Some say she labors through deep winter snows
Up to a single house, and goes inside
To greet affectionately one of those
Who will not die because a dream has died.
Still others say she does no traveling,
Does not arrive when prayed for or required,
Is unaware that she is anything
Which might by those not chosen be desired,
And, dutifully attentive to a few,
Has not the least concern for me or you.

The Abductors

They come as secretly as dreams at night
To stand near doorways or upon the stairs
Almost like guests, congenial and polite,
Whose eyes alone insist that you are theirs.
All you have valued must be left behind:
The picture of the summer path; the bed
Where love was; mystical books that brought to mind
Great images of cities for the dead.
Perhaps you are aware. Perhaps you dial
Emergency for help. Perhaps you throw
A window open, shouting desperately while
They seize you, hush you, leave with you — although
A brave policeman rushing in will tell
Reporters you are there, alive and well.

Glass

It's been around for centuries. One would think
Some evolutionary cleverness
Would send those wasps to freedom at a chink
Between the cabin boards — not to distress
In mindless exploration on the glass
Of windows where they haplessly alight,
Supposing it the pleasant space they pass
When opened doors allow them to be right.
But with their sad insect persistence, they
Restudy and restudy what they know,
And if, by chance, they lift themselves away,
It's only to another pane they go,
As though, with narrow liberty in view,
Their instinct says, "Wide light will let us through."

Her Portrait

In his mid-thirties Corot, who would remain a bachelor, painted a
portrait of Alexina Ledoux, an employee in a family business.

Might it be love? It pleased him when she came
Up from his mother's shop to watch him paint.
She paused on entering, standing in the frame
Of the open door, her face showing a faint
Smile half-hinting that she thought of him
In moments of her own. When asked to pose,
She seemed delighted, and arrayed her slim
Figure in opulent blue and scarlet clothes.
Might she have love in mind while sitting there
Hour after hour, as his sure hand and eye
Intently moved her to a canvas where
She could be held for an eternity,
Not in his arms — impossible — but yet
In space beyond the reaches of regret?

Paint

Van Gogh said that his *Crows in the Wheat Fields* was an expression of "sadness and extreme solitude."

    I am sad and lonely, but my brush
    Does the swift work that it was trained to do.
    Here is an ordinary field. The hush
    Of autumn is upon it. And yet, through
    Images — the road that goes nowhere,
    The sky darkening dangerously for storm,
    The crows whose black shapes sit like lead in air —
    All is transfigured into uniform
    Expression of myself. The things I see
    Cease to have existence of their own,
    But mirror my inmost reality;
    Even the intimate canvas has become
    Strange to me, as if that flat world knows
    Nothing except its paint. Not fields. Not crows.

Two Bronzes by Barlach

In his heaven, the angel hovers on chains
Although the garment, drawn down by the weight
Of bronze, says only spiritual force restrains
His falling from that sweet, ecstatic state
Where his hands hold himself, and where his eyes
Have closed themselves against the least surprise.

On his earth, the singer's legs are folded
Under himself, and steady him for song.
The bronze secures him in his clothing, molded
To body that will never not be young.
His eyes close, as the open lips declare
His music's exaltation into air.

Barlach made them, quietly making clear
"Our death is here," and then, "Our life is here."

IV
At Home

Doing Dishes

With supper done, with piles of plates and pans
Lining the kitchen counters, the routine
Of washing seems to call like destiny;
So with an almost spooky willingness
I do the glasses, dishes, silverware,
And cooking pots — exactly in that order.
I couldn't have said why, but Baudelaire
Explained it in a preface to his poems:
That one of everyone's "immortels besoins"
Is for *monotony*. The world survives,
Perhaps, because we need to do the dishes.
For when a second need of ours, *surprise*,
Begins to itch at people or at nations,
Look out! Who knows what tons of crockery
May crash to floors before surprises end,
Before the rubble can be swept from kitchens,
Before the cooking fires can be relit,
Before the washing water can be heated,
Before monotony can be restored.

Roses

During the night of fever, as she lay
Between an exhausted wakefulness and sleep,
I sat beside her fearfully, in dismay
When her slow breathing would become so deep
It seemed that she might slip beyond recall.
Then I would touch her; then she would revive;
Then, when her eyelids opened and a small
Smile would greet me, hope would come alive.
With morning, the ordeal was over. Gone
Was every trace of illness. A soft rain
Had swept across the countryside at dawn,
So even our garden was made fresh again.
Then Janet went among our roses where
She and the roses shone in luminous air.

Touches

The imperceptible flattenings at the ends
Of fingers, little dentings when I press,
Fleeting sensations as my hand descends
Along your back, moments of happiness —
As when you pass me with a touch so light
I wonder, "Did it happen?" though my arm
Has come alive to pleasure from the slight
Almost-not-contact; or those times your warm
Smile says that all is well, a cold is gone,
There is no danger, and upon the lips
We kiss again, while the new day takes on
A summer aura — then I think, perhaps
Such fragile happenings have to do with love . . .
Hardly worth notice, hardly worth speaking of.

Sunday Sermons and Sonnets

For now we see through a glass, darkly.

— 1 Corinthians 13:12

"Today's text . . . ." Father found his in The Book,
And from that text was drawn, as through a die,
A subtle golden argument that took
The listener deep into philosophy,
Where sin was darkness, where we were in sin,
But faith, and hope, and charity could bring
Us all to glimpse the true light, and begin
To know sure solace for our suffering.
Today's text . . . mine has come from where he pressed
Indelible sentences into my brain,
Providing figures for a mind distressed
When faith has been unable to sustain
The son whose sight can find no way to pass
Beyond a silvered, self-reflecting glass.

Maluku in Cornish

The onyx eye looks sideways at me. What-
Cha doin', whatcha doin'? — the half-squawks
Ask what I ask myself. He takes a nut
I cannot crack and cracks it. Now he walks
Along my arm and up my shoulder. There
He sways and preens like any cockatoo
In rain-drenched trees in soft Spice Island air.
His beak combs through my hair. What will we do
With winter at each window? Will we find
The solace sometimes given as a gift
When two so separate minds are of one mind?
He beats his wings. I feel a little lift
And for a moment gaze across a bay,
A native harbor, half a world away.

Perspective

I stand, and look, and see where I am now.
The sloping street is inches deep in snow.
Because traffic must have its way, a plow
Will surely come along; its blade will throw
A sheet of scrapings sideways with a roar,
Shaking the ground beneath me. I'm aware
Though, now, that someone I have known before —
A neighbor — blocks away appears to stare
In my direction. I am in a town
Where I may, an observer, be observed,
Captured in image, even noted down
In words. "He stood at Fiddle Lane and served
To demonstrate how distance makes men small.
I saw the face. The name I can't recall."

Jogging with Tanya

There are disadvantages, for Tanya
Is curious about other things than I am —
Smells in bushes, rubbish, other dogs
Barking as though she threatened to attack them,
And evidence that horses came before us.
Nevertheless, we run mostly together;
When I pull on her leash, she usually
Will leave whatever stopped her, uncomplaining.
My interests are more cosmical than hers are:
I ponder human suffering on the inclines,
The universe's beauty on the downgrades,
The way life is an uphill-downhill matter,
And how it can be told of in iambics.
I like to think I am the more amused,
And that my speculations will be valued
By gods whose work of health I am assisting
With my exertions, though they are exhausting,
And though when we turn finally at our driveway
We both are glad to walk, and I am sweating.

A Guardian Tanya

Guardian animals . . . adorn tombs in every civilization,
accompanying the soul on its crossing of the river of death.
— Kenneth Clark, *Animals and Men*

Sensing when I must travel, she refuses
To sleep downstairs. She comes into the bedroom,
Nuzzles her biscuit bone into a corner,
Circles twice, and lies down at my feet.
Her sleep is sound, and I sleep soundly too,
As if we two were sculptures in an abbey,
Memorialized by a forgotten artist
Who understood necessities of friendship.
It's likely she will die before I die,
And though I have no faith in streets of gold,
I have half-confidence that I will meet her
On this side of a bridge across death's river,
Letting arriving spirits pat and scratch her,
Or stretching out, her head between her paws
As if for sleep, but with her eyes wide open,
Watching, waiting, sure that I will get there,
Sure that I will find her among thousands,
Coming gladly with a leash to link us
So we can go to death as on a walk.

Acknowledgments

The author is indebted to Dana Gioia for friendly counsel, to John Irwin for his assistance with choosing the poems included here, to Jane Warth for her meticulous editing, and to all of those at the Press who have helped bring *Fiddle Lane* into being.

Some poems in this book appeared in the following periodicals, to whose editors grateful acknowledgment is made.

Antioch Review: "Two Bronzes by Barlach", © 1983 by The Antioch Review, Inc. *Antioch Review*, vol. 41, no. 3 (Summer 1983).

Beloit Poetry Journal: "The First-born."

Boulevard: "A Couple in the Café de la Gare."

Free Lunch: "The Inseparables at the Rink," "Talking with Charlot," and "Maluku in Cornish."

Kennebec: "Casting the Nets" and "Basho's Journey."

Poetry: "Creation," "The Monster in the Park," "Daedalus Invents God," "A Picture of the Reverend's Family with the Child of One," "Catching Fireflies," "Her Diamond Ring," "Even the Weariest River," "A Conversation," "What People Make," "On Sitting Down to Read the Dust Jacket Once Again," "Burning Her Past," "Nobody at Treblinka," "The Abductors," and "A Guardian Tanya."

Portland Review of the Arts: "In the Garden," "Tom and Stone," "New Life," "Wedding Feast," "That's a Nice Leg," "Ill in Babylon," "Dante in the Market," and "Doing Dishes."

Texas Review: "Perspective."

"A Picture of the Reverend's Family with the Child of One" also appeared in the 1984 edition of *Anthology of Magazine Verse and Yearbook of American Poetry*. "What People Make" appeared in the 1987 edition.

Thomas Carper, with his wife, Janet, and baritone friends, has performed Renaissance a cappella trios in live and broadcast concerts in New England and France. His poems have appeared regularly in *Poetry* and other journals.

Fiddle Lane

Designed by Ann Walston

Composed by Blue Heron, Inc.
Goudy Old Style with Caslon Open Face display

Printed by Thomson-Shore, Inc.,
on 60-lb. Glatfelter B-16